Happy Birthday Bugs

This Looney Tunes Library Book is published by Longmeadow Press
201 High Ridge Road, Stamford, CT 06904
in association with Sammis Publishing

With special thanks to

Guy Gilchrist • Jim Bresnahan • Tom Brenner • Mary Gilchrist
Ron Venancio • John Cacanindin • Mike Micinillio • Frank McLaughlin
Allan Mogel • Gary A. Lewis

Printed in the United States of America
0 9 8 7 6 5 4 3 2 1

DAFFY DUCK
and
PORKY PIG

in DUCKS OF YORE

DAFFY DUCK and PORKY PIG
in
DUCKS OF YORE

written by Gary A. Lewis

Illustrated by
The Guy Gilchrist Studios

"J.L.!" Daffy Duck rushed into his producer's office. "I've got to talk to you. You're killing my career with these comedy pictures! Comedy! Always comedy! Honest, J.L. You've got to give me a dramatic part. I've got to play a dashing, romantic hero in a big historical epical drama. My fans demand it!"

9

"And it so happens," Daffy went on, "that I have got the very script that we've been looking for. You'll love it, J.L. It's got swash. It's got buckle. It's got adventure and excitement. You won't regret it, J.L. Just wait and see. I'll be brilliant. They'll line up at the box office to see me."

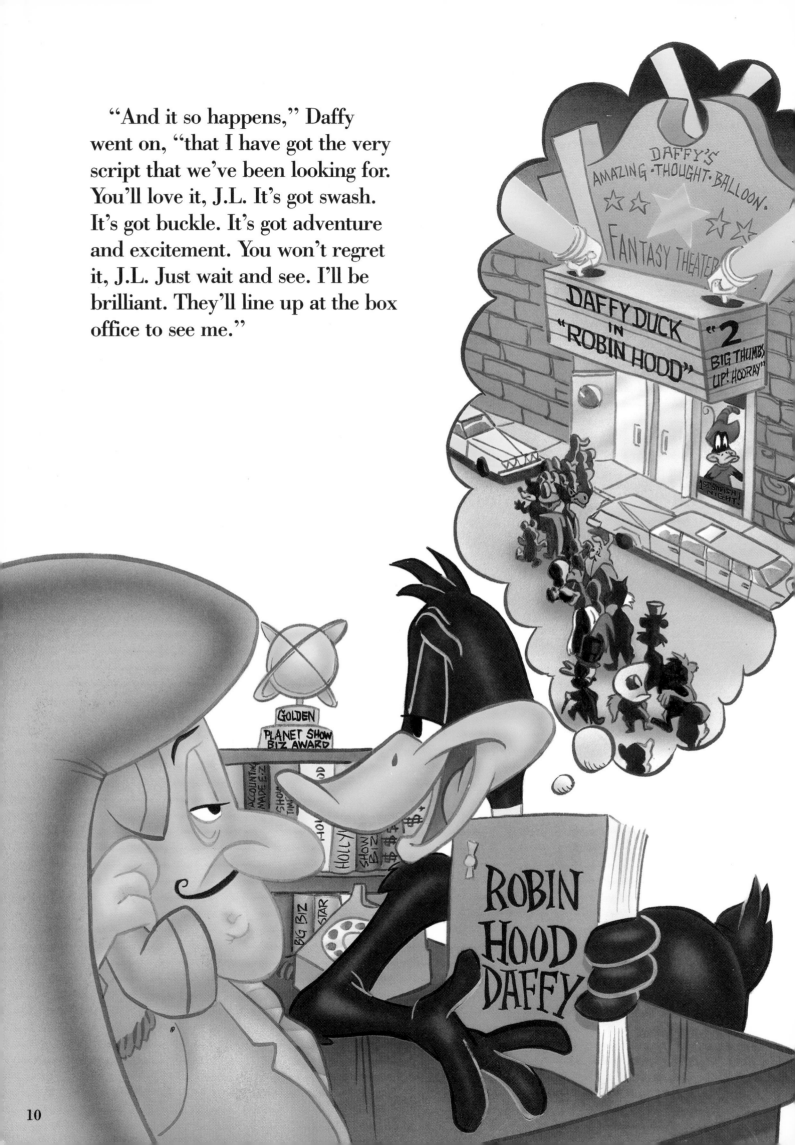

In Sherwood Forest many years ago lived a brave outlaw known as Robin Hood. The Sheriff in those days was an evil man, who had taken away Robin's lands and title. Robin had been driven from his home and forced to live in the woods, where he robbed from the rich to give to the poor.

But despite his hardships, Robin Hood was a merry soul. He always had a song on his lips and a twinkle in his eye. He spent his time tripping merrily through the forest. Unfortunately, he sometimes didn't look where he was tripping.

This particular day, while tripping through the forest, Robin Hood happened upon another merry-looking soul named Friar Tuck. Friar Tuck loved a good laugh, and Robin Hood was certainly something to laugh about.

"It's not *that* funny," sputtered Robin Hood. But Friar Tuck just laughed and laughed some more.

Friar Tuck may have been overcome by the sight of Robin Hood, but Robin Hood, on the other hand, was not amused.

"Ho ho and ha ha, will you?" said Robin. "I'll ho-ho you, my fat friar—with my trusty quarterstaff!"

WHIRRR

Robin Hood whirled his staff. "You'll notice my fantastic technique," he told the good Friar. "I'll teach you to laugh at Robin Hood!"

But what Robin didn't know was that in addition to loving a good joke, Friar Tuck loved a good fight.

Robin Hood was clever with his staff. He parried and thrusted. He dodged and spun. He turned and guarded. But he was still no match for Friar Tuck. With one swipe of his little twig, the Friar sent Robin into a tailspin.

"Y-y-yipes!" yelled Robin Hood as Friar Tuck neatly dumped him into the stream once more.

After Robin had climbed out of the water, Friar Tuck addressed him. "Oh traveling clown," said Friar Tuck. "Couldst thou d-d-direct me to Robin Hood's hideout? I would j-j-join me up with his band of merry outlaws."

"Friar! I am he for whom thou seekest!" cried Robin Hood happily. "I am Robin Hood!"

"Oh, c-c-cut it out," said Friar Tuck. "If you don't know where Robin Hood is, just s-s-say so."

"But truly!" cried Robin Hood. "I *am* Robin Hood!"

"S-s-sure you are," said Friar Tuck. "And I'm the B-B-Big Bad Wolf."

Friar Tuck turned to leave, but Robin stopped him. "Wait!" he said. "Give me a chance! I will prove to you that I am Robin Hood, bravest outlaw ever to live in Sherwood Forest!"

Robin grabbed a rope that hung from a tall tree. He swung himself toward Friar Tuck, intending to land in front of him. But instead of catching the Friar, Robin ran into a little trouble.

Once Robin had recovered, he raced after Friar Tuck.

"I'm Robin Hood, and I'll prove it to you," he insisted. "See yon rich, unwary traveler? I'll rob him of his gold, and then give it to some poor unworthy slob. That'll prove that I'm Robin Hood. Hmm? Okay? Hmm?"

"All right, j-j-jester," said Friar Tuck, sighing. "Do thy worst."

"Good. Watch as I send yon arrow through his wishbone," Robin Hood declared, loosing his bow.

"I'm w-w-watching," said Friar Tuck. "I'm watching."

Robin let an arrow fly. But instead of the arrow winging its way toward its target, Robin found himself in mid-air. Then he found himself mid-tree.

"I'm having bad luck with these trees today," he muttered. "But I remain unboughed."

27

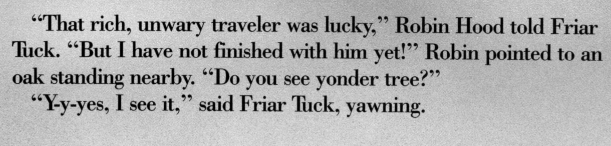

"That rich, unwary traveler was lucky," Robin Hood told Friar Tuck. "But I have not finished with him yet!" Robin pointed to an oak standing nearby. "Do you see yonder tree?"

"Y-y-yes, I see it," said Friar Tuck, yawning.

"Well, I have tied my rope to its branches, and now I will fly though the air toward my target!" Robin declared. "I will capture his gold before you can count to three."

"One… two…" Friar Tuck responded.

"Three." Friar Tuck finished counting as Robin Hood grasped the rope and jumped. "Yoiks, and away!" he cried, as he flew through the air toward his target.

Unfortunately, another tree got in his way.

"That's why they call it a forest," Friar Tuck explained, shaking his head.

"Join me," said Robin Hood woozily, "and I'll convince you I'm…
I'm… who did I say I was, anyway?"

"I am s-s-sorry," Friar Tuck replied. "But I c-c-can't join you. I'm c-c-convinced that you're just not Robin Hood."

"Okay," said Robin Hood. "I give up. Never mind joining me. I'll join you. Shake hands with Friar Duck!"

And the two lived merrily ever after in Sherwood Forest.

Robin Hood didn't do very well at the box office. But Daffy wouldn't give up.

"Here it is, J.P.," he said, bounding into his producer's office one morning. "This is the script for me. *Robin Hood* was just a warm-up. This is the picture that's going to make me a great dramatic star!"

"Now," Daffy went on, "where to begin? Aha. Here on page one. 'Once upon a time'—great beginning, huh?—'Once upon a time, in Merrie Olde England, there lived a daring young highwayman known as the Scarlet Pumpernickel.'"

The Lord High Chamberlain's men could never catch this daring desperado… for he was slippery as an eel and smart as a fox.

The Lord High Chamberlain was simply furious. Milady Melissa was simply delighted. You see, she was in love with the gallant Pumpernickel.

But the Chamberlain had forbidden her to see her hero.

One day, the Lord High Chamberlain had a brilliant idea.
"I will m-m-marry Milady Melissa to the Grand Duke. That will
bring the Scarlet Pumpernickel to t-t-town… and then I will capture
him and imprison him in my d-d-darkest dungeon!"
"Quick!" he called to his secretary. "Take a letter to the Grand
D-D-Duke."

The Grand Duke received the
letter with mixed emotions.
  "I am happy, for I am to marry
the fair Melitha," he said. "But I
am altho furious, because I
despise the Thcarlet Pumpernickel."
Then the Grand Duke brightened.
"I know. I'll carve up the
Pumpernickel and have him for
breakfatht ...and then
marry Milady Melitha. That will
make me feel much better!"

Meanwhile, high in a tower room, the fair Melissa awaited her fate—while everywhere, the Lord High Chamberlain's men lay in wait for the Scarlet Pumpernickel.

"Oh, my darling Scarlet," she cried. "Now we'll never be wed!"

Meanwhile, at an inn on the other side of town, a weary young nobleman had just alighted from the Dover coach.

"Do you have a meal and a room for a weary young nobleman?" he asked the innkeeper.

"Oh, Mr. Nobleman," replied the innkeeper. "You honor my humble wodgings."

"They are humble," the nobleman agreed, "aren't they?"

That evening, the young nobleman paid a visit to the Lord High Chamberlain. He requested an audience with the fair Melissa. But before he could see her, the Grand Duke rushed into the room.

"We mustht have the wedding tonight!" he cried. "I have heard that

the Thcarlet Pumpernickel is about." He turned to the young nobleman. "And who might you be?" he asked.

"Perhaps I am the Scarlet Pumpernickel of whom you speak," replied the young nobleman.

The wedding took place later that night. But there was one uninvited guest.

It was…the Scarlet Pumpernickel!

"Save me, Scarlet!" cried Melissa. "Save me!"

"I will save you, Milady Melissa!" the Scarlet Pumpernickel assured her.

"After them!" screamed the Lord High Chamberlain. "They must not ge-ge-ge-escape!"

"Halt!" The Grand Duke barred the way. "If you want the fair Melitha, you will have to fight me!"

"Must I?" asked the Scarlet Pumpernickel.

"You mustht" replied the Duke.

"Well, in that case…she's yours," said the Scarlet Pumpernickel.

"Scarlet!" cried Milady Melissa.

"Oh, all right," said the Scarlet Pumpernickel.

"Take that, you despicable Duke, you!" cried the Scarlet Pumpernickel, pulling out his sword.

"And take that, you theedy Pumpernickel!" snarled the Grand Duke.

"You haven't got a chance," said the Scarlet Pumpernickel. "You're the villain in this picture, and you know what happens to villains!"

Blades flashed. Melissa gasped.

Clink! Clash! Fence! Fence! Fence!

A great battle raged between the Grand Duke and the Scarlet Pumpernickel.

For awhile, it looked like the Grand Duke was getting the better of the Scarlet Pumpernickel. But the Scarlet Pumpernickel neatly flew out of harm's way.

That's when the fair Melissa stepped between them.

"You horrible man!" cried Milady Melissa, kicking the Grand Duke in the shins. "Look what you've done to Scarlet. Take that!"

"Ouch!" cried the Grand Duke. "Ouch! All right! If you want to marry the Thcarlet Pumpernickel that much…marry him!"

And so, the Scarlet Pumpernickel rescued the fair Melissa from the Grand Duke…and they lived happily ever after.